and Other Anagrams

Collected and Illustrated

by Jon Agee

A Sunburst Book
Farrar, Straus and Giroux

To Winced Poet and Tepid Debt*

THE COUNTRYSIDE

ON ANY SCREEN

HOT CEREAL FIASCO

THE NUDIST COLONY

NO
UNTIDY
CLOTHES

ULYSSES
S. GRANT

THE
ARCHEOLOGIST

HE'S GOT A HOT RELIC

ESKIMOS

SOME SKI

A PSYCHIATRIST

THE U.S. LIBRARY OF CONGRESS

DR 5·7 →
← CL2B

IT'S ONLY FOR RESEARCH BUGS

GROWN

WRONG

THANK
YOU VERY
MUCH

Almost all of the anagrams included here were found in books, journals, or through friends. In many cases the original source of a specific anagram was unclear or unknown. Some of them were created before the twentieth century, others as recently as 1999. What follows is a list of authors with the anagram(s) they created: Josefa Heifetz Byrne (SOUTHERN CALIFORNIA/HOT SUN, OR LIFE IN A CAR); Mrs. Henry Eagleton (THE COUNTRYSIDE/NO CITY DUST HERE); Don Emmerson (LIONESSES/NOISELESS); Darryl Francis (THE U.S. LIBRARY OF CONGRESS/IT'S ONLY FOR RESEARCH BUGS); Theodore Funk (POETRY/TRY POE); William Grossman (THE EYES/THEY SEE); Robert Hooke (THE ARCHEOLOGIST/HE'S GOT A HOT RELIC); William Lawrence (A SENTENCE OF DEATH/FACES ONE AT THE END); Kathryn Ludlam (NORWEGIANS/SWEN OR INGA); E. J.

McIlvane (LIFE'S AIM/FAMILIES and COMMITTEES/COST ME TIME!); Carrol Mayors (A DECIMAL POINT?/I'M A DOT IN PLACE!); O. V. Michaelsen (ON ANY SCREEN/SEAN CONNERY?); Morton L. Mitchell (SLOT MACHINES/CASH LOST IN 'EM); Norman Nelson (THE NUDIST COLONY/NO UNTIDY CLOTHES); Laura Olkowski (SCHOOL CAFETERIA/HOT CEREAL FIASCO; LIFE ON MARS?/ALIEN FORMS!; NICE SEAT/I CAN'T SEE; and REST IN PEACE/A SINCERE PET); Arthur Pearson (ROAST TURKEY?/TRY OUR STEAK); and D. C. Ver (THE ANSWER/WASN'T HERE).

Thanks also to John Baumann, my aunt Rena, O. V. Michaelsen for providing most of the author credits, Laura Olkowski, Mark Saltveit, Will Shortz, and John D. Williams, Jr., the executive director of the Scrabble Association, for suggesting this book in the first place.

BIBLIOGRAPHY

Charles Carroll Bombaugh, *Oddities and Curiosities of Words and Literature* (New York: Dover Publications, 1961); Dmitri Borgmann, *Language on Vacation: An Olio of Orthographical Oddities* (New York: Scribner, 1965); A. Ross Eckler, *Making the Alphabet Dance* (New York: St. Martin's Press, 1996); R. J. Edwards, *The Longman Anagram Dictionary* (Essex, England: Longman, 1985); Willard Espy, *Garden of Eloquence*: A *Rhetorical Bestiary* (New York: Harper & Row, 1983) and *An Almanac of Words at Play* (New York: Clarkson N. Potter, 1975); Patrick Hughes, *Words at Play* from *The Paradox Box* (Boston: Redstone Press, 1993); O. V. Michaelsen, *Words at Play: Quips, Quirks & Oddities* (New York: Sterling Publishing Co., 1997).

*To Pete Cowdin and Deb Pettid

Levi's is a registered trademark.

Library of Congress Cataloging-in-Publication Data

Agee, Jon.
    Elvis lives! : and other anagrams / Jon Agee.
        p.   cm.
    ISBN 0-374-42095-5 (pbk.)
    1. Anagrams. I. Title.

PN6371.5.A335   2000
793.734—dc21
                              99-38139